Stin

Megan McDonald

illustrated by

Solar System Superhero

Peter H. Reynolds

SCHOLASTIC INC.
New York Toronto London Auckland
Sydney Mexico City New Delhi Hong Kong

ISBN 978-0-545-38028-7

Text copyright © 2010 by Megan McDonald.
Illustrations copyright © 2010 by Peter H. Reynolds.
Stink®. Stink is a registered trademark of Candlewick Press, Inc.
All rights reserved. Published by Scholastic Inc., 557 Broadway,
New York, NY 10012, by arrangement with Candlewick Press.
SCHOLASTIC and associated logos are trademarks and/or
registered trademarks of Scholastic Inc.

12 11 10 9 8 7 6 5 4 3 2 1   11 12 13 14 15 16/0

Printed in the U.S.A.   40

This edition first printing, September 2011

This book was typeset in Stone Informal and hand-lettered.
The illustrations were created digitally.

Lexile is a registered trademark of MetaMetrics, Inc.

for Luke and Cash
M. M.

To my brother, Andy Reynolds
P. H. R.

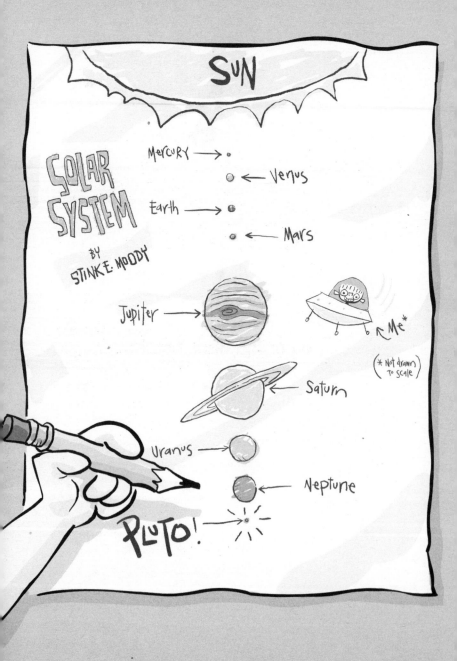

CONTENTS

Move Over, Saturn   1

Vroom! Vroom!   11

Extra Credit   21

Miss Space Camp Know-It-All   37

Jupiter Jerks   51

Short Stuff   67

Urp!   77

No-Good, Rotten Recess   87

Pluto Rising   101

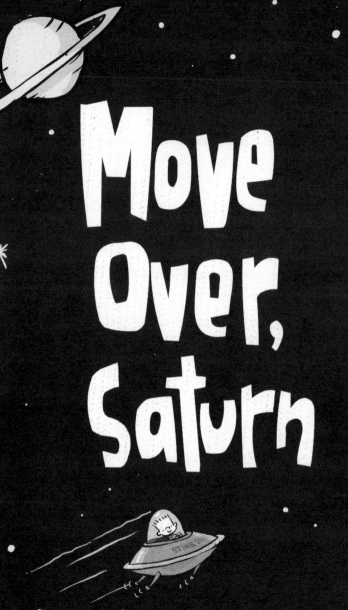

Flub!

Flop!

Flunk!

Stink Moody had to take a test. A super science test. A solar system test. He had to learn all the planets . . . by tomorrow!

Stink went to find his big sister. He sure hoped Judy wasn't in a mood. If Judy was moody, Stink hoped it was a help-your-little-brother-study-for-his-test mood.

There were nine whole planets, and Stink only knew about one. The one in the *S* encyclopedia: Saturn. You might even say Stink was a Super Saturn Expert.

Saturn had rings and moons and was made of gas (hardee-har-har). Saturn could float like an ice cube in a giant's bathtub (if you just happened to know any giants). Saturn could spin so fast, it looked flat as a silver-dollar pancake, Stink's favorite food on Earth-not-Saturn.

One year on Saturn took 29 Earth

years. If Stink was 7 on Saturn, that would make him 203 years old on Earth! Way older than Judy!

*　*　*

Stink found Judy in her room, on her top bunk, making a picture out of Already-Been-Chewed gum.

"What's that?" Stink asked.

"It's a Venus flytrap made out of ABC gum," said Judy.

"You know what would be even cooler?"

"What?" Judy asked.

"A picture of Saturn made out of ABC gum," said Stink.

"Who cares about Saturn?"

"Me," said Stink. "But now I have to care about eight other planets, too."

"Huh?" Judy looked up from her ABC-gum art.

Stink held up his science book. "I have a test tomorrow. A big fat test on the planets. Will you help me study?"

"No way, Stinkerbell," said Judy. "Can't you see? I'm way busy."

"But you're so smart," said Stink, buttering her up.

"That's not what you said when I had to get a math tutor."

"But you've been to second grade, right?"

"Stink, I've been to college!"

"See? I need somebody super smart, smarter than second grade. I need somebody college-smart to quiz me."

"Do I get to boss you around?"

"Sure," said Stink.

"Do I get to yell 'Hardee-har-har' if you flunk?"

"I'm not going to flunk," said Stink, "because you, my super-smart sister, are going to help me." He pushed the science book over to Judy.

Judy flipped through the book. "Name the nine planets."

"Too hard," said Stink.

"You have to know the names of the planets. Mrs. D. is going to ask that for sure. Think, Stink."

Stink closed his eyes. "Saturn . . .

Jupiter . . . Earth . . . Pluto, and that one that comes before Pluto."

"Stink, good thing you have me, your brainy big sister, to teach you. My Very Excellent Mother Just Served Us Nine Pizzas."

"I thought Dad was making us spaghetti."

"No, Stink. That's how you remember the planets. The first letter of each word in the sentence stands for a planet. Mercury, Venus, Earth, Mars, Jupiter, Saturn, Uranus, Neptune, Pluto."

"My Very Excellent Mother Just Served Us Nine Pizzas!" said Stink.

"Your very excellent *father* is just about to serve spaghetti," said Dad, coming into Judy's room. "C'mon, you two. Time for dinner."

"I was just teaching Stink how to remember the planets," said Judy. "Like ROY G. BIV helps you remember all the colors of the rainbow. Mr. Todd says it's called a moronic."

"I think the word is *mnemonic*," said Dad.

"Who thought that up?" said Judy.

"Some *moron*," said Stink. He and Judy cracked up all the way to the dinner table.

✶ MNEMONIC COMICS ✶

M̲ercury

SUN

←

On the bright side
of Mercury, it's a
face-melting **840** degrees!
Don't forget your sunblock! SPF 5000?

On the dark side
of the planet, it's
<u>minus</u> **275** degrees.
Brrrrrrrr!
Better pack your long underwear!

V̲enus

What is the stinkiest planet?
- A.) STINKARON
- B.) VENUS
- C.) P. UPITER

THE ANSWER:
B.) VENUS

Blame it on hazy clouds
of sulfuric acid.

> Smells like a giant
> rotten egg! P.U.!

The next day after school, Stink sat on his race-car bed. He stared at the page with all the Pluto questions. He stared at the big fat red *X*, as big as the Great White Spot on Saturn.

Stink wished he could zoom away on that car bed. Down the stairs and out of the house and up the road and into outer space. He wished his race-car bed would rocket him all the way to the rings of Saturn.

He might as well move to another planet. Anywhere but Pluto.

"What's wrong?" Judy asked when she saw his sour-ball face.

Stink held up his test. He pointed to the big fat red *X*.

"Did you flunk? For real?" Judy asked, grinning.

"You know that thing you taught me? Well, guess what? My very excellent mother DID NOT Serve Nine Pizzas."

"What did she serve?"

"Nothing. Zero. Zip. T. I. N. P. There. Is. No. Pizza."

"What do you mean, there's no pizza?"

"There's no letter *P*. Because there's no Pluto."

"How can there be no Pluto? Where did it go?"

"It's still up there, but it's not a planet anymore. There are only eight planets now."

"Stink, they can't just take away a *whole entire* planet. That would mess with the *whole entire* solar system."

"Well, they did. Ask Mrs. D. She said Pluto is too small, and it has a weird orbit. Besides, they found

14

something bigger, so they flunked
it. Voted it off the island. Kicked it out
of the solar system. Pluto is gonzo."

"Who's *they*?" asked Judy.

"Big important science guys. One
day, the President of Outer Space had a
big meeting and everybody voted and
Pluto got kicked out, so it's not one of
the nine planets anymore."

"What is it?"

"A *dwarf* planet."

"A dwarf planet! So now are they
going to call it Grumpy? Or Dopey?"

"No, but they *are* going to call it
Number 134340."

"What? That stinks on ice," said Judy. "I can't believe Mr. Todd didn't tell us. This is big. Really big! How come Mrs. D. didn't tell you?"

"I guess she did. But I don't think I was even in the room. I think I was at the nurse's office getting my hearing checked."

"Well, you better get it checked again if you didn't hear your teacher say they kicked a whole entire planet out of outer space."

"Pluto's my favorite, too."

"Wait. I thought Saturn was your favorite."

"Next to Saturn, I mean."

"What's so great about Pluto, anyway?"

"Jupiter's the biggest and Mars is the reddest and Venus is the hottest and—"

"Oh, I get it. Pluto is the smallest planet in the solar system, isn't it? And you're the shortest kid in your class. You're both puny. Instead of Pluto, they should call it Punk-o."

"Nah-uh!"

"You just like Pluto because it's so cute-o."

"Hardee-har-har. This is serious. What am I going to do?"

"Face it, Stink. The time has come to find another second-favorite planet."

"But I mean, what about my test? Maybe I can talk to my teacher. But what if she doesn't let me take it over?"

"Talk to her, Stink. You'll just have to explain what happened."

"Easy for you to say. Your teacher isn't a big fat Pluto Meanie."

MNEMONIC COMICS

Earth*

Earth speeds through space at 66,700 miles per hour and weighs

5,972,000,000,000,000,000,000 **TONS!**

That's equal to the weight of 1 sextillion 194 quintillion elephants!

THAT'S A LOT OF PEANUTS!

*Birthplace of STINK E. MOODY!

S cience time!" said Mrs. D. "Let's go over your tests."

Stink took out his test. He tried to cover up the big red X on the Pluto page with his elbow, in case Nick, the new kid in front of him, turned around.

Stink stared at the back of the new kid. His head looked a little like a small, almost-round planet.

Just then, Mrs. D. got a call from the principal. "Okay, class. Everybody take out your math workbooks and open to page 101. Keep working while I go talk with Ms. Tuxedo."

"Teacher got sent to the principal's office!" somebody snickered.

Planet Head Nick turned around. Nick showed Stink his test. Nick had a big fat red *X* on the Pluto page, just like Stink.

"I got skunked!" said Planet Head.

"Me too!" said Stink, lifting up his elbow.

"At my old school," said Nick, "Pluto was still a planet. This is so not fair."

"Tell me about it. I was with the

nurse getting my ears checked when Mrs. D. told about the NO PLUTO rule. And nobody, not even my best friends, Webster and Sophie of the Elves, told me."

"You can call me Skunk, by the way," said Nick.

"And you can call me Stink," said Stink. "I thought I was the only person on the planet with a smelly name."

"Nope. And guess what? I like smelly stuff, just like my name."

"Me too!" said Stink.

"I was in a smelly-sneaker contest at my old school," said Skunk.

"No way!" said Stink. "I got to judge a super-smelly-sneaker contest."

"I smelled a durian fruit one time," said Skunk. "It's like the way-worst smell in the world."

"P.U.," said Stink. "I want to smell a corpse flower someday."

"Freaky-deaky," said Skunk.

"Double freaky-deaky," said Stink.

"At my old school," said Skunk, "back when there were still nine planets in the solar system, my science book had this neat trick about how to remember them."

"My Very Excellent Mother Just

Served Us Nine Pizzas!" Stink and Skunk said at the same time.

"Now they'll have to think up a new one," said Skunk, "without the *P* for Pluto."

"Let's see. . . ." said Stink. "How about, My Very Excellent Mother Just Served Us Nothing!" Skunk cracked up.

"My Very Excellent Mother Just Said U Nerd!" Sophie said, joining.

"Many Vampires Eat Mothballs Just So U Know," piped up Webster.

"Those aren't even the right letters!" said Skunk, chuckling.

"Many Vampires—" said Webster.

"Eat Macaroni Jelly Sandwiches—" said Sophie.

"Unless Naked," Stink finished.

Skunk laughed. "Hey! That doesn't even make sense."

"Wait. I got it!" said Stink. "My Very Educated Monkey Just Spoke Utter Nonsense."

"Good one," said Skunk. "You get extra credit for that one."

"I wish," said Stink. "Hey, we should

make up a new saying for real to remember the planets, including the three dwarf planets."

"You mean Ceres, Pluto, and Eris, too?" asked Sophie.

"My brother says there's another one too, called Makemake," said Webster.

Stink's head was spinning. He wrote eleven letters across the top of his notebook:

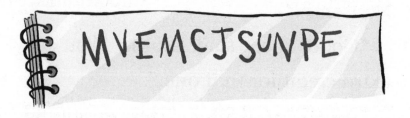

M V E M C J S U N P E

Then scribbled down words:

My Very Eager Mad Cat Just Scratched Up Nose-Picking Earwigs.

Now Sophie and Webster tried.

My Very Edible Macaroni Cheese Just Spit Up Nasty Puking Eyeballs.

Stink and Skunk howled then put their heads together and came up with another saying.

My Very Energized Mystery Car Just Shot Under Nine Police Escorts.

"That is so way good," said Sophie.

✶　✶　✶

When Mrs. D. came back, kids were talking loud and letting the class guinea pigs run loose and shooting

hoops in the trash can. Mrs. D. blinked the lights. She clapped her hands five times. Class 2D took their seats and clapped their hands five times in response.

"Did anybody solve any problems while I was gone?" asked Mrs. D.

Nobody said a word. Stink passed a note to his friends. *Many Virginia Excited Math Children Just Screwed Up Not Practicing Education!*

Skunk shot his hand up. "We did. Stink and I solved a problem."

"Good for you," said Mrs. D. "Which one was it?"

"The Pluto Problem."

"The Pluto Problem?" Mrs. D. flipped through the pages of her Teachers' Edition math book.

"It's not a math problem. It's a science problem."

"Even better," said Mrs. D. "It's time for science anyway."

Stink and Skunk told the class all about the new saying they made up. Riley Rottenberger raised her right hand. She was wearing a shirt that said SPACE CADET and calling, "Ooh! Ooh!" like she had a major stomachache.

"Riley? Did you have something you wanted to say?"

By now Mrs. D. should have known that Riley Rottenberger always had something to say.

"There's a real saying for the dwarf planets," said Riley. "A girl made it up and won a contest, and it isn't about a mystery car or police. It's, My Very Excellent Magic Carpet Just Sailed Under Nine Palace Elephants."

"Thanks for letting us know, Riley. That's very creative. Stink and Skunk came up with a creative sentence, too."

Riley shrugged and made a sour-ball face.

"Boys, come see me after class," said Mrs. D., "and see what we can do about those red Xs."

⋆ MNEMONIC COMICS ⋆

Mars

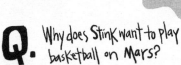

Q. Why does Stink want to play basketball on Mars?

A. BOING! He could jump SUPER high because the gravity on Mars is only a third of that on Earth.

Q. Why would Stink go mountain climbing on Mars?

A. Because Olympus Mons, a Martian volcano, is three times as tall as Mount Everest!

(THAT MUST MEAN THAT A YETI ON MARS HAS THREE TIMES AS MUCH HAIR!)

The next day, Stink was sitting at his own desk minding his own business when Riley Rottenberger waltzed past, showing off her new T-shirt. It did not say SPACE CADET. It did not say SPACE OUT AT SPACE CAMP. It said PLUTO IS DEAD.

"Who *is* that?" asked Skunk.

"Rotten Riley Rottenberger, aka Miss Know-It-All."

Riley turned around. She fake-smiled at Stink and Skunk. "When is a planet not a planet?" she asked them.

"When it's Grumpy?" said Stink.

"When it's Sneezy?" said Skunk.

"No, when it's PLUTO!" said Riley, cackling all the way to her desk.

"Pluto is SO a planet," said Stink. "A dwarf planet."

He turned to Skunk. "She thinks she's so great 'cause she got to go to Space Camp."

"For your information, Pluto is not

a planet anymore," said Riley. "Don't you guys know anything? Oh, I forgot. You never went to Space Camp!"

Riley was right. Stink had never been to Space Camp. He had never tried on a space suit (except one made out of aluminum foil in preschool). And he never got to see inside a spaceship (except the cardboard-box kind).

"Did you get to ride in the gravity chair?" Skunk asked Riley.

"*And* the Five Degrees of Freedom Chair," said Riley. "It floats on air." Stink wished he had Five Degrees of Freedom from Riley Rottenberger.

"Don't ask her questions," Stink warned, "or she'll never, ever stop."

"Why didn't Saturn want to sit next to Jupiter?" Skunk asked anyway.

"Why?" asked Riley.

"Because Jupiter had a lot of gas," said Skunk, holding his nose.

"Hey, no fart jokes in class," said Miss Know-It-All. "Mrs. D. said."

"I have one," said Stink. He couldn't help himself. "Why didn't Saturn's mom want him to take a bath?"

"Why?" said Skunk.

"Because he always left rings in the bathtub!"

"Good one!" said Skunk. Riley ignored them.

"Time to get into groups," said Mrs. D. Stink was on a team with Webster and Sophie of the Elves. He asked Skunk to join them. Each team was making a model of the solar system.

Stink and his team were using Styrofoam balls for the planets. They dipped hunks of raw wool in soapy water. Once the wool was stretchy, they shaped it around each ball to form the outer surface of the planet.

Riley's team was making planets out of fancy clay.

Riley leaned over and pointed to the tiny ball in Stink's hand. "What's that?"

"What does it look like? It's the planet Pluto. "

"Stink Moody," said Riley, "how many times do I have to tell you? THERE IS NO *PLANET* PLUTO."

"Is too," said Stink.

"Is not."

"Is so too."

"Riley, turn around," Webster said. "You're not even on our team."

"I don't see why everybody's so down

RAW WOOL

SOAPY WATER

STYROFOAM BALL

STRETCH WOOL

PAINT

PLANET!

on Pluto," mumbled Stink, adding a touch of purple-gray to his planet. "Pluto's cool. It might be small, but it doesn't just do what all the other planets do. It has its own orbit."

"Yeah," said Skunk. "I don't get why they voted to take it away."

"Because Pluto's puny like a dwarf," Riley butted in. "Pluto gets its butt kicked by all the other planets. If an asteroid came, Pluto would be all 'Aah! I'm scared,' and shrink away."

"Nah-uh!" said Stink.

"Yah-huh. Ask anybody. I learned it at Space Camp."

"Space Camp, Space Camp, Space Camp!" said Stink. "People should boycott Space Camp for telling lies about Pluto."

"Stink! Riley!" Mrs. D. said sharply. "What's going on back there? You're supposed to be working on your Science."

Riley's hand shot up into the air. "This is Science," she said. "That's what we were fighting about."

Mrs. D. came over to their tables. "What seems to be the problem?"

"Riley says there's no Pluto," said Stink, "and I say there is."

"Riley, what makes you say there's no Pluto?" asked Mrs. D.

"You said it yourself!" said Riley. "Pluto got its butt kicked out of the solar system. It's just a number now."

"Riley, I'd rather you didn't say 'butt' in this class."

Stink couldn't keep from smiling when his teacher said *butt*.

"But it's still up there," Stink said, "even if it is a dwarf *planet*."

"Actually," said Mrs. D., "you're both right."

"Huh?"

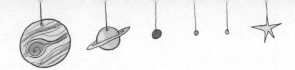

"Scientists argued about it, too. They had to study Pluto for a long time."

"Then they had a big meeting," said Riley, "and voted it O-U-T *out*!"

"Yes, they did," said Mrs. D. "But some scientists still think Pluto should be called a planet."

"YES!" Stink pumped his arm in the air and high-fived his team.

"Tell you what," said Mrs. D. "Why don't we turn it over to our own panel of scientists?"

"You mean we get to be scientists right here in our class?" asked Stink.

47

"Sure. We can have a discussion, a debate next Friday. Riley, your team can explain why you think Pluto should not be a planet anymore. Stink, your team can argue why Pluto should still be a planet. You have exactly one week to prepare your arguments."

"Super Galileo!" said Stink.

Riley narrowed her eyes at Stink. "Stink Moody, you are SUCH a . . . a . . . Pluto Head!"

"Thanks," said Stink, sitting up a little taller.

✳ MNEMONIC COMICS ✳

Jupiter

BIG, BADDER, BEST!

I'M BIGGEST! I'M BADDEST! I'M JUPITER JERK, KING OF THE PLANETS!

BIGGEST: How big am I? Try: As big as **1,300** Earths!

FASTEST: I rotate the fastest of ANY planet in our solar system! A day with me is only **10** hours long!

BADDEST: Check out my Great Red Spot. It's a storm that has been raging for at least **300** years!

P.S. I have rings, too. Take <u>that</u>, Saturn and Uranus!

The following Monday morning, Stink was in a huddle with his friends. "We have to tell everybody about Pluto so they'll vote to keep it in the solar system."

"Let's tell the whole world!" said Sophie.

"The whole galaxy!" said Webster.

"The whole universe!" said Skunk.

Stink's team made up a secret handshake. They each held out a fist

and piled one on top of the other.
"P-L-U-T-O!" they shouted, then waved
their hands high in the air and yelled,
"PLUTO POWER!"

"Look out. Here comes Riley and her
friends," said Skunk.

"Logan, Morgan, and Heather
aren't her friends," said Stink. "They're
just on her team because she let them
touch her space rock."

"Space rock?" said Riley. "It's a hunk of meteor. From Mars!"

"La-di-da," said Skunk.

"What's your team's name?" asked Riley. "The Stink Bombs?"

"What's yours—the Jupiter Jerks?" asked Stink.

"It's WAY more official if you have a name. We're Team Kick-Pluto's-Butt. Team KPB for short."

"No way will Mrs. D. let you use *butt* in your team name," said Stink. "This is a school thing."

"Okay, then we'll be Team Kick-Pluto's-*Behind*. That's still KPB."

"Whatever," said Sophie.

"Stink, you just like Pluto because it's the smallest and you're the shortest," Riley said. "You're always for the underdog, but everybody knows that Jupiter is the best. We even have team shirts!" she said.

Just then, Riley's team lined up beside her, all wearing the same shirts. The shirts did not say SPACE CAMP RULES. The shirts did not say TEAM KPB. The shirts did not even have words. Each shirt had a number: 134340. The number for Pluto, now that it wasn't a planet!

Stink looked down at his shirt. I'M KIND OF A BIG DEAL. He took the top off of a marker and changed it to PLUTO IS KIND OF A BIG DEAL.

"Look! Up in the sky, Stink." Riley pointed. "It's a bird. It's a plane. It's a frog. No, wait. It's a puny ex-planet getting kicked out of the solar system!" Team KPB cracked up. "You should be Team Underdog." Riley Rottenberger sure was rotten. And getting rottener by the minute.

* * *

After school, Stink and his team met in the Toad Pee Club clubhouse, aka the backyard tent. "We need an official name," said Stink.

"How about the Stinkazoids?" said Skunk.

"The Plutonics?" asked Webster.

"The Extra-Extra-Galactic Einsteins?" asked Sophie.

"Maybe Rotten Riley was right for once," said Stink. "We could be the Underdogs. You know, small like Pluto, but we come from behind to beat the pants off the Jupiter Jerks."

"And you could be Captain Pluto, our leader," said Sophie of the Elves.

"Captain Pluto and the Underdogs," said Stink. "I like it!" Everybody agreed. Captain Pluto and the Underdogs made T-shirts for their team. They each drew a flying planet wearing a Superman cape with a capital letter *P*.

"Let's make signs, too," said Skunk.

"'Cuckoo for Pluto,'" said Webster, waving his marker in the air.

"We can march around school and wave our Pluto signs."

"We can have a Pluto parade on the playground," said Stink.

For a long time, all that could be heard in the tent was the squeaking of markers.

At last, the signs were finished. The Underdogs went home. Stink ate supper and thought about Pluto. He took a bath and thought about Pluto. He did his not-science homework and thought about Pluto. Stink Moody, aka Captain Pluto, had Pluto on the brain!

Stink went to bed and couldn't sleep a wink. He sneaked outside to the tent. He shone his flashlight on the signs lined up in a quiet parade. Next thing he knew, a bright light was shining back at him, right smack in his eyes. "Hey!" called Stink, shielding his eyes.

"Stink Moody," said a deep voice, "this is the Pluto police. Come out with your hands up."

But it was not the Pluto police. It was just Judy.

"You scared me half to death," said

Stink. "What are *you* doing out here in the middle of the night?"

"What do you think? I'm spying on what *you're* doing out here in the middle of the night." Judy's flashlight hit the signs. PLUTO IS KIND OF A BIG DEAL. "Wow! Did you guys make all these?"

"Yep. Today. What do you think?"

"I think you have Pluto-itis. You need a Pluto-ectomy," said Dr. Judy.

"I couldn't sleep," said Stink. "Just think," he half-whispered, pointing to the night sky. "Pluto's up there, right now, billions of miles away, just waiting for us to save it. To earthlings, it just looks like a golf ball with dimples. But it's spinning out there with tons of other hunks of rock and chunks of ice. And it needs us."

"And don't forget space junk," said Judy. "You know, the trash astronauts throw away. Like fridges and stuff."

"They don't have refrigerators flying around in outer space!"

"Yah-huh. And paper clips and sneakers and decks of cards and empty jars of Tang and all sorts of stuff."

Judy and Stink tilted their heads back and stared up at the sky.

"Killer rocks are out there, too," said
Stink, "streaking through space. One
could smash into Earth at any second.

A big giant asteroid like the one that wiped out the dinosaurs could be on its way, headed right for Planet Earth."

"Cosmic," said Judy. "You better hope an asteroid hits before Mom and Dad find you out here in your PJs on a school night when you're supposed to be in bed."

Stink and Judy headed back to bed. But before they did, Stink turned off his flashlight. He held two fingers up to the sky. "*Urp!*" he said. "We come in peace."

✴ MNEMONIC COMICS ✴

Saturn

I'm Saturn!
Lord of the Rings!

I've got bling. How many ringlets do I have?
Tens? Hundreds? Thousands!

What are my rings made of?
DIAMONDS? GOLD? **NO!** Billions of bits of ice
and rock, some as small as a grain of sugar,
some as big as a **car**!

How fast do they spin?
So fast I'm dizzy just thinking about it!

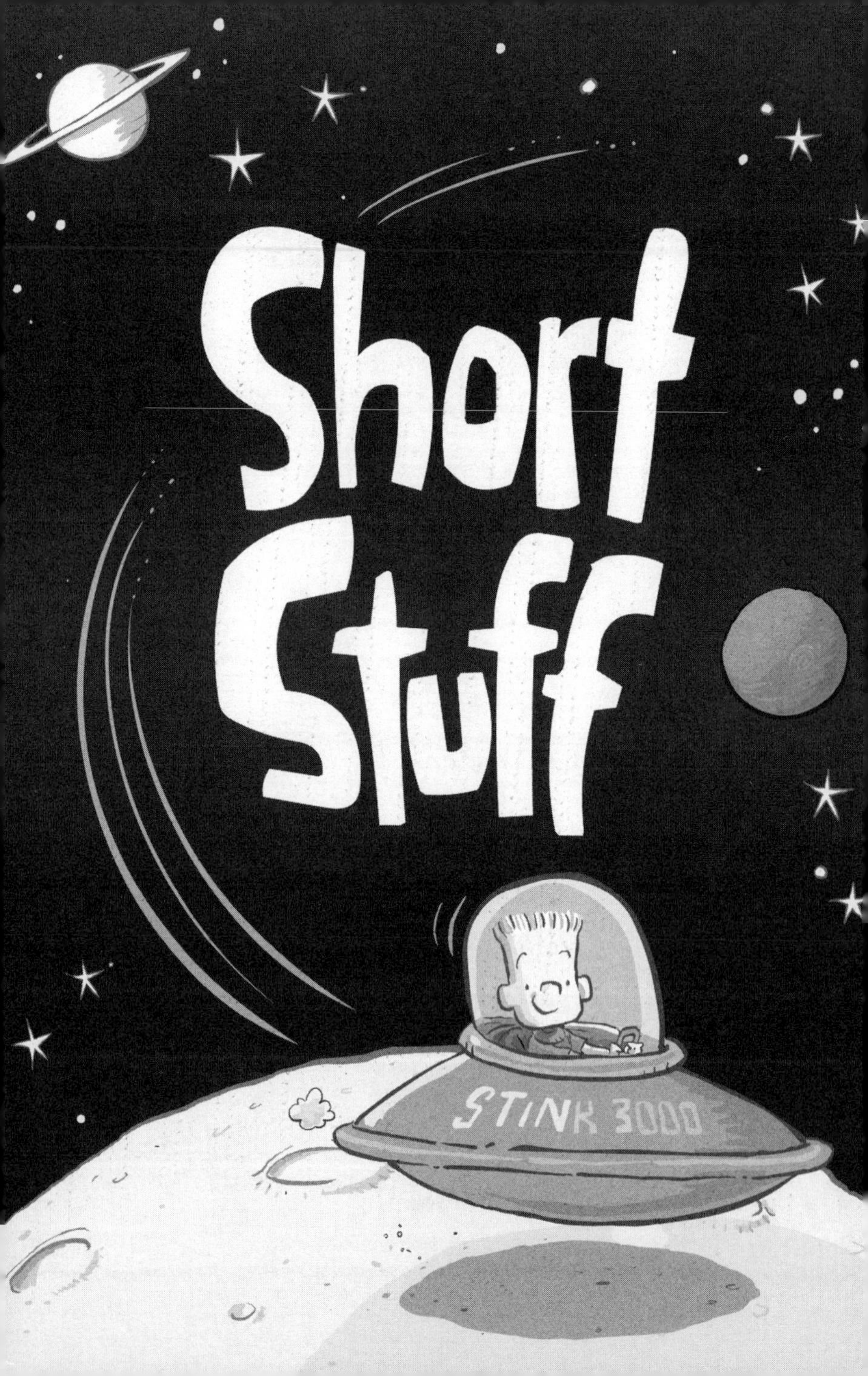
Short Stuff
STINK 3000

Early the next morning, Stink's team stood out in front of the school. As the buses pulled up, Captain Pluto and the Underdogs waved their signs.

Rotten Riley marched up to Stink, hands on hips. "School hasn't even started yet," she said. "Mrs. D. said we could do this only during *recess.*"

"Who can wait?" said Stink.

Riley turned and stomped away. "Oh, you just wait. I'll get you for this, Stink Moody."

"That's *Captain Pluto* to you!" yelled Stink.

"And the Underdogs!" yelled the Underdogs.

* * *

At recess, Captain P. and the Underdogs waved signs again. They shouted stuff. They even sang songs. *"R-E-S-P-E-C-T! That's what Pluto needs from me,"* Stink sang at the top of his lungs.

"Give me a *P*!" Skunk yelled. "Give me an *L*! Give me a *U*! Give me a *T*! Give me an *O*! What have you got?"

"PLUTO!" yelled the Underdogs.

"I can't hear you!"

"PLUTO!" screamed the Underdogs. Soon nearly half the whole playground was screaming, too.

Then out came Rotten Riley and the

KPBs. They were dressed in black from head to toe and carrying shovels.

"Are they wearing *garbage bags*?" asked Sophie. Sure enough, Riley and the KPBs had on black garbage bags with holes cut where their heads and arms poked through.

Somebody yelled, "Who forgot to take out the trash?"

"We're not trash," said Riley. "We're dressed in black because we're going to a funeral."

"Huh? Wha?"

"FYI, Pluto died. Pluto is D-E-A-D dead."

Then Riley and her rotten team began to dig in the dirt, but they were not planting a garden. They were not searching for buried treasure. They were digging a grave. A grave for Pluto!

"We've been skunked!" said Skunk.

Riley took out a tiny plastic ball. "Pluto is officially dead," she said, dropping the ball into the hole and covering it over with dirt.

"Good-bye, Pluto," said the KPBs. "Sure, we'll miss you. But you're not a planet anymore."

When they were done, they put

up markers in the dirt, like at a pet cemetery.

"Moment of silence, please," said Riley with a serious face. A hush fell over the second-grade crowd, and the playground was dead silent.

HERE LIES
PLUTO
ONCE A PLANET
R. I. P.
1930 - 2009
PLUTO'S BUTT GOT KICKED HERE.

Stink felt like he was in a black hole. He couldn't help it. He spoke. He broke the spell. "Pluto is SO not dead, Riley Rottenberger!"

Stink walked away at warp speed, leaving a dust tail behind him.

URP!

✷ MNEMONIC COMICS ✷

Uranus

They call me the
ICE GIANT!

 ~ BRRRRR!
URANUS IS THE COLDEST PLANET!

SUN
2 BILLION MILES THAT WAY
Neptune Express

It's always winter up there. Wicked winds blow, and clouds made of ice crystals hang around in the atmosphere.

The surface temperature is about minus **300** degrees!
No wonder! Uranus is almost 2 BILLION miles from the sun.

Stink had to think, think, think. He had to think up a way-smart Pluto plan. A rottener-than-Riley plan. Something that would convince Class 2D and Mrs. Dempster that Pluto wasn't dead. But what?

Stink fed Toady. Stink talked to Astro. Stink drove and drove and drove. His car bed, that is. All the way to outer space.

Stink's race-car bed was covered with tons of bumper stickers.

Stink stared at the bumper stickers. Suddenly he saw them in a brand-new way.

Faster than you can say "Ratbert" (the Mars rock, not rat), Stink had an idea. A plan.

Stink took out the Make Your Own Magnetic Bumper Sticker kit that he had gotten from Judy for his birthday. He made a brand-new bumper sticker.

A perfect Pluto bumper sticker.

All he needed now was a bumper. Stink knew just the bumper and just the car for Operation Bumper Sticker.

Now all he needed were the Underdogs. His team. A few good friends to be his lookouts.

✳   ✳   ✳

The next morning before the bell rang, Captain Pluto and the Underdogs met under the big maple tree by the teachers' parking lot.

"Listen up," said Stink. "It's not just a plan. It's more like a mission. You know, to help Pluto."

"Yeah, Mission Impossible," said Webster. "Impossible that you won't get caught and get in big trouble."

"I won't get caught," said Stink. "That's why I have you guys."

"Okay, we're in," said Skunk, starting the secret Pluto handshake.

"I just need you guys to be on the lookout while I sneak up to the car," said Stink. "Make sure no teachers are coming."

"We'll be like spies," said Webster.

"Outer-space spies," said Sophie.

"If a teacher comes, yell out the secret code," said Stink.

"What's the secret code?" asked Skunk.

"*Urp!*" said Stink. "Just say '*Urp*'!" He grinned. "Okay, places everybody." Skunk hid behind the tree. Webster ducked behind a trash can. And Sophie crouched behind a bench.

Stink looked left. Stink looked right. The coast was clear. He scooted across the parking lot. He ducked behind a green car, darted beside a black van, and scooched over to a blue Mini.

He pulled the bumper sticker from his back pocket and, in a split second, stuck it to the blue Mini's bumper: HONK IF YOU LOVE PLUTO.

"*Urp!*" Sophie called in a loud whisper, but Stink didn't hear.

"*Urp! Urp! Urp!*" yelled the others.

Stink stood up.

Right smack in front of Stink was a teacher. A tall teacher.

Judy's teacher, Mr. Todd.

"Hello there, Stink," said Mr. Todd.

"Hi, Mr. Toad—I mean Todd," Stink croaked.

"Checking out the Mini, huh? Great little car. Roomier than it looks. I've been thinking about getting one of these guys myself. Saves on gas."

"Yeah, gas," said Stink, backing up to stand in front of the top-secret super-sneaky bumper sticker.

"Well, we'd both better be getting to class, don't you think?"

"Yeah, class," said Stink.

Stink and Mr. Todd headed for the front door, followed by three super-sneaky, second-grade outer-space spies.

Mission Impossible had just become Mission Accomplished.

MNEMONIC COMICS

Neptune
IS THE MATH PLANET!

1846

Neptune was first seen through a telescope in 1846. Before that, math wizards figured out that it was up there!

3,000,000,000

Approximate number of miles from Neptune to the Sun!

16 Number of Earth hours in a Neptune day

165 Number of Earth years in a Neptune year

2010

Hooray! In 2010, Neptune will have made it around the sun for the first time since its discovery!

11 Number of moons Neptune has

I'll pay you back next Neptune year! URP!

No-Good, Rotten Recess

On Thursday, Mrs. D. announced, "Everybody take out your science books. Turn to page sixty-seven."

Stink lugged the heavy book out of his desk. He opened to page sixty-seven. Stink could not believe his eyes. "Hey," he said, looking around. "Mrs. D.! Something's not right."

"Somebody wrote all over my science book!" called somebody else.

"Me too!"

"Me three!"

"Somebody crossed out all the Plutos!" shouted Stink, looking around at all the other books.

"Boys and girls," said Mrs. D., "let's just keep calm." She walked around the room, up and down the aisles, looking at everybody's books.

"The Evil Science-Book Fairy strikes again," said Sophie of the Elves.

"Anti-Pluto goblins are on the loose," said Webster.

"Now, class, you know we don't go

around writing in textbooks. Would anyone like to tell me who did this?"

"Yeah, whoever did this sure is *rotten,*" said Stink, glaring at Riley.

"Okay, okay," said Riley. "I did it."

"Riley, you know better than this. What were you thinking?"

"Well, Pluto's not a planet anymore. So I crossed it out—when everyone was at recess."

"I thought we agreed we'd hold a debate on Friday."

"We did, but I had to do something. Even you've already taken sides."

"No one's taken any sides," said Mrs. D. "I'm leaving it up to all of you. Class 2D will debate and decide for themselves, fair and square."

"Then why are you driving all over town getting everybody in the whole world to honk for Pluto?"

Mrs. D. looked confused. Heather Strong pointed out the window at a little blue Mini parked outside. Mrs. Dempster's little blue Mini.

Mrs. D. leaned and peered out the window at a mysterious bumper sticker on her car. HONK IF YOU LOVE PLUTO.

She couldn't help smiling. "So that's why everybody's been honking at me since yesterday!"

"See?" said Riley. "I rest my case."

"Riley, I didn't know anything about it until just now. I think we may have a Bumper Sticker Bandit in Class 2D."

"And I bet his name is Stink Moody!" said Riley, pointing.

"Stink," asked Mrs. D., "do you know anything about this?"

"I might," said Stink. "Okay, I did it!"

"Boys and girls, I know we're all enthusiastic about the subject of Pluto. But you know better than to go around writing in schoolbooks and sticking bumper stickers on cars without asking permission. Riley, Stink, I'm disappointed in you both."

"Sorry," said Stink.

"Sorry," said Riley.

"Stink, first of all, I'm going to need you to go peel off that bumper sticker at recess."

"It's just a magnet," said Stink. "It's not even stuck!"

Mrs. D. nodded. "And you and Riley are going to spend recess erasing all the marks in the books."

This was going to be a no-good, rotten recess. The rottenest.

✳   ✳   ✳

Stink zoomed around the room, desk by desk. He erased book after book after book. He made a pile of eraser crumbs. A blizzard of eraser crumbs. A mountain of eraser crumbs.

Glancing across the room at Riley, Stink asked, "Did you know that before they had rubber for erasers, they actually used bread crumbs?"

Riley didn't say a word.

"Did you know that the eraser was invented more than two hundred years ago?"

Riley didn't say a word.

Stink erased some more. "How many erasers do you think it would take to circle Planet Earth?"

"Stink Moody, you are so e-noying!"

"E-noying? Is that like annoying with an e-raser?" Stink laughed at his own joke.

"FYI, Mr. Eraser Head, e-noying is extremely annoying."

"Did you learn that at Space Camp?"

"For your info, it's none of your beeswax." Riley rubbed her eraser superhard. "I was never in trouble before, and now I'm in trouble and I have to stay in at recess, and it's all because of you, Stink Moody!"

"I'm not the one who scribbled all over the science books! I don't see why you hate Pluto so much. What did Pluto ever do to you?"

"Don't you get it?" said Riley. "You're just like Pluto."

"Why? 'Cause I'm short? I have gas? What?"

Rotten Riley, Queen of Space Camp,

looked like an Oort cloud about to explode. "No, because you're always crossing my orbit!"

"Okay, okay," said Stink. "You don't have to go all asteroid on me!" *Wicked wormholes!* Sometimes Riley Rottenberger was just plain extra-terrestrial, maximum warp-speed, supernova annoying!

STINK 3000

Pluto
Rising

At last it was Friday. Time for the Class 2D scientists to present their cases!

Team KPB went first. Riley held a wooden spoon in the air. "Today we are here to decide if Pluto is a planet. I'm a Solar System Supreme Court judge. This is my hammer thingy." *Bang!* Riley rapped the wooden kitchen spoon on Mrs. D.'s desk.

"It's called a gavel," said Mrs. D.

"There are three laws, like tests you have to pass, to be a planet."

Morgan and Heather walked in neat circles around a yellow beach ball marked SUN. Logan was walking funny around the beach ball.

"Hey, Pluto, why are you walking funny?" Heather asked Logan.

"I can't help it, Neptune. My orbit's out of whack," said Logan.

"Law Number One," said Riley. "To be a planet, you have to orbit around the sun.

"Law Number Two. To be a planet, you have to be big and round, or else you get pushed around by the other planets."

"Pluto is almost round," Stink pointed out.

Bang! "Odor in the court!" Riley said by mistake. Everybody cracked up.

"Law Number Three. To be a planet, you have to be big enough to kick rocks and other space junk out of the way."

Logan bumped into Morgan. Logan bumped into Heather. But they did not budge. Not one inch.

"Pluto is way too puny to bump stuff out of the way. Therefore," said Riley, using a big word to sound super-duper smart, "Pluto is NOT a planet. No way, no how."

Logan (aka Pluto) shrank to the ground, took off his sweatshirt, and showed off the T-shirt he had on under it. It said, 134340.

"I rest my case." Riley hit the desk with the spoon so loud it sounded like the Big Bang. "Vote NO for Pluto. It's the law."

"Let's give Riley's team a big hand," said Mrs. D. Everybody clapped. "Next up is Stink's team with a short play."

CAST

 Neptune . . . Skunk

 Saturn . . . Sophie

 Jupiter . . . Webster

 Pluto . . . Stink

 Neptune: I'm Neato Neptune, the Blue Planet.

 Saturn: *(Twirling two Hula-hoops.)* I'm Spinning Saturn. I have rings!

 Jupiter: I'm Jupiter Jerk. I'm the biggest of them all.

Pluto: *(Flinging Superman cape in air.)* I'm Captain Pluto! I may be small, but — *(Pluto bumps Neptune. Neptune bumps Saturn. Saturn bumps Jupiter.)*

Neptune: *(Staggering.)* It's too crowded in this solar system. Too many planets!

 Saturn: But we've always had this many planets.

 Jupiter: One of us has got to go.

 Neptune: Not me.

 Saturn: Not me.

 Jupiter: Not me.

 Pluto: Well, don't look at me. What did I do?

 Jupiter: You're too small.

 Saturn: You're not round enough.

 Neptune: And you have a weird orbit.

 Pluto: But I'm roundish. And I never bump into you very hard, Neptune, do I?

Neptune: We don't care. Get out of our solar system.

 Saturn: Find your own Milky Way.

 Pluto: *(Goes into corner and cries.)* Waah-hah-hah.

 Saturn: Uh-oh. Pluto is crying.

 Neptune: He must be lonely.

 Jupiter: Maybe he misses his friends.

Riley: No way! Don't let him in!

Mrs. D.: Riley, you had your turn. Let's hear them out.

Saturn: I feel bad. I think we should let Pluto back into our solar system.

 Jupiter: I vote yes.

 Neptune: I vote yes.

(Skunk, Sophie, and Webster walk over to Pluto and pull him out of the corner.)

 Saturn: C'mon, Pluto. We were wrong to kick you out.

 Neptune: You can be with us in the solar system.

 Jupiter: We're all part of the same family: the Milky Way.

 Pluto: *(Skipping, dancing, and singing.)* We are family! Jupiter, Saturn, Neptune, and me! We are family! I got all my planets with me!

Class 2D went wild. Stink and his fellow planets took a bow.

"Nice job," said Mrs. D. "Now, let's see what the rest of Class 2D thinks. We'll put it to a vote."

Everybody took out their pencils and secretly scribbled down their votes. They dropped them into a big jar. Mrs. D. sat at her desk, unfolding slips of paper. She came to the last vote. Slowly, she unfolded it. "Looks like it's unanimous. We all agree. Class 2D votes YES for Pluto to still be a planet." Everybody clapped and hooted.

"The *whole* class? Are you sure you counted right?" asked Stink.

"I'm sure," said Mrs. D., winking at Riley. Riley smiled back, a not-so-rotten smile.

"Woo-hoo! Pluto lives!" Stink yelled.

"Let's hear it for Stink, Solar System Superhero!" called the Underdogs.

Stink beamed, proud of all the kids in his own little solar system, Class 2D.

After school, Stink went to find

smiley Riley. "Hey, Riley, um, I was just wondering, what made you change your mind about Pluto?"

"None of your beeswax," said Riley. Still rotten.

Stink started to walk away.

"It's just . . . I know how Pluto feels," Riley mumbled.

"Huh?"

"At Space Camp—"

"Here we go again," said Stink, rolling his eyes.

"This isn't a brag. For real. I was going to say, at Space Camp, the other kids said I was extremely e-noying.

113

They kicked me out of our bunkhouse. So, when you were in the corner crying—"

"*Pretend* crying," said Stink.

"Whatever. I know how Pluto feels. To be kicked out, I mean."

Stink could not believe his ears. Maybe Rotten Riley was not so rotten after all. "At Space Camp, do you get to launch super-duper monster rockets and make robots?"

"Of course. And the robots rescue astronauts on the Space Station."

"Wow." Stink had only ever dreamed of Space Camp. "Hey, we should start a new club. Friends of Pluto or something."

Riley twirled her hair into a knot. "You mean, just for your friends?"

"Any friend of Pluto is a friend of mine," said Stink, grinning.

* * *

Just then, Judy came to the door of Stink's classroom. "C'mon, Stinker. Mom's picking us up today. I have soccer, and you have karate."

"See you later, ex–Pluto Hater," Stink said to Riley, and they both cracked up. Stink grabbed his stuff and hurried down the hall after Judy.

Judy climbed into the backseat.

"I'll be right there," Stink called.

"What's he doing?" Mom asked, looking in the rearview mirror.

"I think he dropped something," said Judy. "Stink. Hurry up! I'm going to be late!"

Stink scrambled into the backseat.

Mom pulled away from the school and took a left turn. At the first red light, a car honked.

"I wonder why they're honking," said Mom. "I'm sure I had my turn signal on." As they drove on, another car honked. And another.

Honk, honk! Toot, toot! Beep!

"Mom, do you know them?" Judy asked. "They're all waving at us."

"Here a beep, there a beep, everywhere a beep, beep!" sang Stink, smiling to himself. Someday, a spaceship would travel to the planet Pluto, 2.7 billion miles away. Someday.

But today, Stink was happy. Happy to be here on Croaker Road, State of Virginia, Planet Earth, Milky Way Galaxy: His own little corner of the universe.

Beep, beep!

Megan McDonald _____

is the author of the popular series starring Judy Moody. She says, "Once, while I was visiting a class, the kids chanted, 'Stink! Stink! Stink!' as I entered the room. In that moment, I knew that Stink had to have a book all his own." Megan McDonald lives in California.

Peter H. Reynolds _____

is the illustrator of all the Judy Moody books. He says, "Stink reminds me of myself growing up: dealing with a sister prone to teasing and bossing around—and having to get creative in order to stand tall beside her." Peter H. Reynolds lives in Massachusetts.